D1758773

This book is for you

Oxford University Press, Great Clarendon Street, Oxford OX2 6DP

Oxford New York
Athens Auckland Bangkok Bogota Buenos Aires
Calcutta Cape Town Chennai Dar es Salaam
Delhi Florence Hong Kong Istanbul Karachi
Kuala Lumpur Madrid Melbourne Mexico City
Mumbai Nairobi Paris São Paulo Singapore
Taipei Tokyo Toronto Warsaw

and associated companies in
Berlin Ibadan

Oxford is a trade mark of Oxford University Press

Text copyright © Margaret Connolly 1997
Illustrations copyright © Rosita Manahan 1997
First published 1997
First published is paperback 1999

A CIP catalogue record for this book is available
from the British Library

ISBN 0 19 279916 9 (hardback)
ISBN 0 19 272367 7 (paperback)

Printed in China

It Isn't Easy

Margaret Connolly

Illustrations by Rosita Manahan

Oxford University Press

My big brother died last year. His name was Ross.
He was nine years old.
   It's been a long time since then, but sometimes I still feel
so cold and lonely. It's a funny mixed-up feeling.

It all happened so suddenly. Ross ran out after our ball, right in front of a car.

   We never thought it would ever happen to any of us.

   No one ever talked about dying.

It should have been me chasing after that ball.

   Now there are only three of us. Me and Mum and Dad.

   I'm the only child left now and it's not easy.

When I said goodbye to Ross before the funeral, he didn't look dead. But he was so still.

The day of his funeral was a horrible day. I felt empty and cold all over.

Afterwards I kept thinking I could hear Ross talking and
singing. I listened and listened, but there wasn't a sound.
No one was there. I must have been dreaming.

Some things haven't changed. Everything in our house
is still the same. Every day I play out on the street with
our friends. But Ross isn't there.

I want him back so badly.

I had so much fun playing with him.

Sometimes I hate Ross for hurting us and leaving us behind.

None of my friends seem to understand how I feel. They don't even talk about him very much.

Even my mum and dad seem different now.

Why did he have to die?

Most people get time to grow old. But not Ross. He was unlucky.

Why did my grandad get to be seventy?

It's not fair.

Sometimes I lie in bed and listen to the wind at my bedroom window. I want to kick and scream and stamp my feet, just like I did when Ross hid Sally, my best teddy bear.

I miss Ross, even though we used to fight.

I remember the fights and the arguments. The time I pulled his hair and he pulled mine back! I remember it hurt for ages afterwards.

And there was the day he blew out all the candles on my birthday cake. I was so cross and angry, and I felt all mixed-up inside, just like now.

But I wish we could have the good and bad times over again with Ross.

I remember all the fun and laughs we had together, too. The day we both ran after Dad, and he slipped and fell in the mud. We couldn't stop laughing.

Or the time after the picnic when we hid in the bushes for hours and hours and no one could find us. It was good fun keeping quiet and listening to everyone calling us.
  Having a big brother was fun.

And I'll never forget the day we
both won a prize in the three-legged
race at the school sports day.
  We liked being together.
  They were good times.

I still do all the things I used to do when Ross was alive.
    I go to school.
    I go swimming.
    I visit Gran and Grandad.
    Sometimes I even have fun.

    My teacher says everything has to die, that dying is one of the most natural things in the world.
    The leaves on the trees die and fall off.
    Usually, we grow from being small babies to big people. But not Ross.

My teacher kind of understands. She is very patient with me.
    Sometimes I am naughty in school, and I do silly things.
    Other times I am sad and quiet.

Some days I paint very angry pictures.
  I paint all over the page and make a terrible mess. And I
don't care. I'm all empty and hollow inside.

Other days I paint happy pictures for my mum and dad. We
play lots of games together and are having a good time again.
  I have got used to being an only child –
but it isn't easy.

Often I cry together with my mum and dad when we look at photographs of the happy times we had with Ross. Then they hug me and I hug them.

I don't understand why he had to die, and I don't think they do either.

I still wonder why it had to be him.

There isn't any answer.

I wish it had never happened, but at least we can talk about him now and remember.

When his anniversary came around, we had a special cake for
Ross and I blew out all the candles. Dad took a photo of me,
and Gran and Grandad came too.
    It was like his birthday, only different.

I often used to wonder, would Ross ever come back?
    We all have a picture of him in our bedrooms.
    It's good to remember him.

It's good to know the truth, but it isn't easy. I know Ross is dead and he won't be coming back.

I'm glad that we were good friends most of the time.

I think he knows I loved him. I will never ever forget him. Neither will my mum and dad.

He'll always be part of us.